A Mouthful of Bread

Secrets of a Dancing Girl

by Cecily Riley

A Mouthful of Bread
Secrets of a Dancing Girl

Text©2018 Cecily Riley

ISBN 978-1-908577-75-7

5 3 1 2 4
First Edition

All rights reserved

British Library Cataloguing in Publication Data.
A catalogue record for this book is available from
the British Library.

ISSN 2515-1568

Conditions of Sale
No part of this book may be reproduced or
transmitted by any means without the permission of
the publisher.

Although loosely based on related events, any
reference to persons, living or dead, is purely
coincidental.

Hawkwood Books 2018

To every naughty girl in this world

Shaking my umbrella in front of Maurice's lodge, I heard the girls laughing chatter. They always seemed to feed off each other's gaiety and their riot was quite potent and intoxicating. They were *all* there, I noticed with a little alarm. I was late again, and not entirely comfortable with that, but still took time to exchange a few pleasantries with the robust Frenchman.

Two things I had learned in my short life that aren't written in schoolbooks: 'Always make friends with the accountant' and 'Always make friends with the janitor'. Maurice was neither, but he was staff so I invested time in keeping on his good side, although sometimes the effort seemed wasted because he was just so bloody nice to everyone. All the same, I always greeted him properly when he was in his lodge and bought him Christmas presents.

To be honest, I quite enjoyed my little chats with Maurice. Like me, he had a past. Like me, he was accustomed to luxury. And, like me, he seemed condemned to stay forever on the outskirts of it. We had a lot in common and a similar world view, which meant we understood each other's jokes and references. We talked about most anything.

I walked down the corridor leading to the brightly lit dressing room, bracing myself for the hours ahead. It was the first night for three brand new numbers, including two dance routines, one of which involved tap dancing to the tune of 'Sweet Georgia Brown'. Considering how ungifted a tap dancer I was, I felt tremendous relief when Mrs Bartlett decided that the second group was going to perform it. She had looked at me queerly, maybe remembering the last time she'd decided to put me in a tap dance routine. I'd tried to muddle my way through, smiling endlessly, but she'd very soon exiled me to the back row. Group choreographies were not my forte. This was going to be a long week.

I put my winning smile on and walked into the dressing room. Somewhat disappointed that no one marked my arrival, I went straight for my dressing table whilst acting busy and aloof. I was especially sad about Mary, conversing in hushed tones with Helen. Considering the thing she was soon to ask of me, I feel it would've been appropriate to be a little more polite.

Jane, already in her lollipop costume of red and white stripes, interrupted her conversation with Ethel and turned to me. I was happy to have such a lively girl as my dressing table neighbour. Ethel was noticeably vexed at being ignored thus and got up to talk to Rachel, 'accidentally' bumping into the back of my chair. As I was about to pick a fight with her, I felt Jane's hand on my arm and saw her shaking her head. She was reminding me that there was no point in getting mixed up with the likes of Ethel. She would get her comeuppance one way or the other.

I was reminded that Jane had as strong a personality as me and that her powerful presence made me look a lot more normal. She bore her Scottish ancestry on her head, by way of a proud red mane and in the rolling 'r's which made every word she said sound more important and more truthful, somehow. I smiled at our connivance.

"Don't worry! With such an ugly soul, she won't last very long."

"What have you planned for her?" I asked in a scheming tone.

"Me? Nothing! But Segomo will find her."

"Who?" I asked, puzzled by her frequent reference to obscure Celtic gods.

"Segomo! The god of war!" she said gleefully.

Looking over my shoulder, I saw Ethel, standing, and Rachel, sitting, both staring at us in the reflection of Rachel's make up table mirror. The look they gave us made me shudder. What had I ever done to provoke such animosity? But then I tended to attract the jealous or otherwise disagreeable type.

"I hope you're right," I sighed as I took off my coat and dress.

It was the first of June but the weather was apparently unaware and stayed on the April showers setting.

"What's with you? Rough night?" Jane asked as she stared at my reflection in the mirror.

"Yes, actually," I smiled, almost tempted to blush. "My canary has circles under his eyes."

"Good for you," Jane cheered as she focused back on her own reflection and make up.

I wondered whether she meant it. She was with another man practically every night, happy to share with us the piquant details of her bed hopping the day after in the dressing room. But was she happy or did she strive for a more steady relationship? I was about to venture into that line of questioning when Mrs Huff walked in.

Whether summer, autumn or winter, she invariably wore her tweet jacket and skirt, a brooch of arguable taste pinned over her left bosom. This consistent wardrobe, other than being cheaper, conveyed a sense of security to us girls. Some things in this mad world, and those mad times, were forever. Her husband, the theatre financier, wore clothes just as dull. If one didn't know them, one would've thought them accountant and housewife, certainly not proprietor and artistic director of one of the most successful revue theatres in the West End.

"Miss Lucy! How good of you to join us!" Mrs Huff, standing in the door, towering over me.

I didn't even try to come up with a clever answer and gave my most endearing smile. She smiled back briefly, as if to say, 'I am watching you,' and went for her inspection tour.

She checked Helen and Little Mary's red and white costumes for 'The Good Ship Lollipop' dance number. Bridget, Greta and Tina were shimmering in their black see-through kimonos, although only Tina managed to look Asian. Bridget's red hair and Greta's blonde locks were quite out of place. We counted four black haired girls but Mrs Huff hadn't been keen on breaking us up so she put blondes in black kimonos. Norma and Rachel were also wearing the Asian statues outfit, much to Mrs Huff's satisfaction. As she passed my table, she glared at me for not looking like a human shaped bonbon yet, and left. Ethel wasn't ready either but she had avoided that confrontation by slipping away, staying out of sight behind the costume rack that parted the room.

Upon our illustrious leader's exit, Ethel threw on her costume and applied her make up with quick, knowledgeable gestures. One thing can be said about Ethel, she was a pro. Then again, she had started awfully early. I knew little about her childhood but had been told it had been particularly rough, that she had to earn her own living by the time she was fourteen… and she wasn't doing that mending clothes. She had an aquiline face with lots of sharp angles and an even sharper gaze. She wasn't the most intelligent girl but her dark almond shaped eyes, fired up by fiery rage, were frightening to us and irresistible to men. So I am told.

"Her heart is in the right place," Jane said,

noticing my staring at Ethel's preparations.

"If only her spine was," I said, as I started to apply my makeup.

That's when I noticed that Jane had decided to take the red and white lollipop theme to the next level, making her face look like a clown's, waiting for Mrs Huff's last check before the show to be over.

I smiled, shaking my head, glad to be surrounded by so many characters. According to my habit, I lingered behind in the dressing room, wanting a moment's peace and quiet before the show, the mighty, awesome tidal wave about to crash upon us.

I was closing my eyes and breathing, basking in the warm glow of all the reflected light bulbs, when my personal little genie materialised beside me. I had grown accustomed to it, to the point of being quite fond of her.

"Hello Lucy. Sorry if I didn't greet you before but Helen was telling me about her childhood."

"I know," I said, opening my eyes and smiling at my friend. "Impressive, isn't it?"

"Yes! Gosh, Lucy, he had a pony!"

"And a maid, a cook and a tutor."

"I didn't know there were people with that kind of money who weren't royalty."

"She is related to them, I think, a cousin or something, twice removed… who isn't, these days?"

"What? Really?" she exulted.

"Well… yes! But please don't faint, we have a show to do," I added as I got up and herded her towards the stairs.

"No, but that's incredible! Does she get invited to Buckingham Palace? Has she been to any balls?"

"Oh, you know, they're not all that grand. Once you've seen one, you've seen them all."

"How would you know? Have you been to any balls at Buckingham Palace?" she sneered.

"Yes, actually," I snapped, and then I remembered that part of my life had to remain hidden. "I mean… no!"

"Which is it, yes or no?"

"No, of course I haven't."

"And do you think Helen has been invited to weddings?"

"No, I don't think so," I said, practically pushing Mary upstairs. "Even less so now that her family has disowned her because of how she carries on."

"They can't do that!" she said, grabbing the oversized lollipop Mrs Brown was handing out to us before we got onstage. "I am sure the day she wants to come back they will welcome her with open arms."

"Yes," I said sarcastically as I went looking for my mark, "and they'll have a big garden party on the palace's lawn."

"Do you think we will be invited?" Mary asked, eyes wide in astonishment.

"No, of course not, you lamb," I winked at her just before the band struck the first chord of 'On the Good Ship Lollipop' and the curtain rose.

I am glad to say that the number went well, as well as can be expected considering how sweet and innocent the routine was and the audience's lukewarm reception, and we hurried backstage to change. The stagehands crossed paths with us under the blue light and went to set up the Asian décor. Mrs Huff was aware of the somewhat haphazard nature of her geographical references but neither she nor her audience cared.

As the others were standing on their marks, a

temple and a junk boat to be precise, and the Asian music started, we changed into our skimpy kilts and white blouses for the Scottish gigue. Mrs Brown came to collect the lollipops while we laughed and chatted quietly. She too possessed the gift of appearing silently out of nowhere. I assume she must have heard a few juicy secrets that way, but I had never heard anyone being scolded by her. According to the Black Cat Theatre's lore, she and Mrs Huff had met under somewhat unsavoury circumstances so they had an unspoken arrangement and kept each other's secrets.

"How's your 'young man'?" Mary asked, sitting in the dark beside me, lacing her shoes.

"Fine," I said, as I struggled with the clasp of my skirt.

"That's all you have to say about it?" Mary asked, disappointed, even a little worried.

"We're fine," I said, trying to sound reassuring. "What about your young man?"

For about a month now, she had been seeing a rather dashing constable by the name of Mortimer Cooper. He had been a member of our audience only once and Mary had met him on the only night she had ever agreed to go into the auditorium after the show. It was a match made in heaven. Both of them were equally awkward and timid but they seemed happy and that was all that mattered. Apparently. Our conversation strayed towards the trappings of binding one's life to only one gentleman.

Soon the curtain came down on the Asian tableau. I felt Jane, Helen and Ethel standing behind me, their chests, pressed in tartan corsets, heaving in the excitement of the coming number. As soon as the other girls had run by us, we followed the stagehands and watched them strike one set and set up another, ready to take our positions.

When the backdrop looked more like a Scottish glen then a Japanese sailor harbour, the orchestra opened with 'Strip the Willow'. The curtain rose and we started hopping away, like a group of coordinated bunny rabbits in skirts, feet pointed, kilts flying in any old direction.

After about a minute, the other group of girls joined us onstage. That's when the number really came into its own, with all ten of us turning and twisting, arm in arm, hand in hand, skipping and bounding. The audience was clapping along joyfully and some of the Scots among them sang along. On the last chord, we stood stark still, in a human pyramid formation. The curtain dropped to the sound of thundering applause as we cautiously came down, with a helping, if wandering, hand from the stage technicians.

Then it was my group's turn to change, necessarily approaching the speed of light. We were supposed to have three minutes but the orchestra knew the set up and the costume change took longer than that. Mrs Huff chided every employee, Maurice included, once a week regarding the length of that 'quick' change but we all bore it, knowing only too well it could not be shortened, Mrs Huff included.

Once the set was up, we would strike the various poses of average ocean liner passengers, assuming it had been a nudist ship, of course. Sunbeds, parasols, deck chairs, straw hats, the props abounded, the clothes not so much. When the last one of us, usually Mary, had let the last of her transparent silk 'towels' artfully drape itself around her torso, the curtain rose.

Confronted with such a vision of golden sunshine, faraway travels and statuesque beauties, the audience went wild. The whistles, the laughter, the applause, the hooting, it sometimes felt like it would never end. But the set, with the boat on top, only revolved twice, slowly. The orchestra eventually got to the end of 'Alone with my dreams' and the curtain dropped. I was almost as disappointed as the audience.

That night, as we ran backstage, we were quite surprised to find the area behind the stage curtain entirely empty. We asked the stagehands, passing us by to strike the boat and set the city skyline, if any of them knew where the other girls were. That's when the smell of smoke came to my awareness. I had started smelling it much earlier, when I was reclining on the deck of the ocean liner's chaise longue, basking in the sunlight of a hundred tungsten light bulbs. But it hadn't permeated the deeper parts of my brain. I suppose that when one faces a rowdy audience wearing absolutely nothing but a smile and large sunglasses, one has to attain a certain state of mind, one that apparently delays the panic caused by the smell of burning scenery.

Because that was the smell that I was now following to the back of the theatre.

There we found Mrs Huff fuming, her arms crossed over her ample bosom. She was facing Rachel in her torn and singed sparkling costume; Norma, Tina, Greta and Bridget, thankfully unharmed and sparkling silver in the darkness, looking very glum; two stagehands with empty buckets in their hands, water still dripping from them, and one pane of the Scottish glen, now adorning a dark, gaping hole.

"What happened?" I asked, expressing the thought of the girls in my group standing anxiously behind me.

"Girls," Mrs Huff said calmly, "go and do the routine. Rachel, you stay here."

The four girls ran onstage, the stage hands having managed to change sets. As the cheerful tune of 'Sweet Georgia Brown' started, and the clip-clop of their tap-dance shoes filled the stage, Mrs Huff turned to me. To this day, I don't know why she told me but I suppose that, in spite of my lack of punctuality and dozens of missed rehearsals, she considered me an employee as opposed to 'one of the girls' who only passes through, looking for something better.

"Rachel thought it would be a good idea to

wait for her turn on stage by lighting a cigarette. Here. Backstage."

We all stared at Rachel as if we had found out she had drowned a kitten. Some of the rules in the theatre have more to do with superstition than with actual proven hazards and we were all smokers. But there was one rule you never broke and that was to go to the roof terrace or the sidewalk to light a cigarette. Putting your colleagues at risk, not to mention the patrons and maybe even the neighbours, was a cardinal sin.

The sentence was swift.

"Rachel, take off your costume, go down, take your things and go. I don't want to see you ever again. If anybody asks, I will tell them you were a good dancer but a dreadful companion in this company."

Mrs Huff spoke to Rachel, looking at her over her shoulder, as if talking to a dog.

Rachel, her chin high and her eyes blazing daggers at all of us, took off her clothes and vanished like a pale ghost into the darkness. I wish I could say we were sad to see her go but her demise had been like all her time with us – so dangerous and volatile, it put us all at risk.

After we had recovered from the first shock,

we rushed to dress for the curtain call. That week, Mrs Huff had picked out a skimpy little red number with enough sequins to dazzle our admirers into buying another bottle of champagne while they waited for us to appear amongst them, or so they were led to believe. All nine of us bowed, shook our bottoms at the audience and vanished like a naughty, sparkling dream.

Which brings me to the next 'dreamy' event of the evening.

Or so it should. But I forgot to mention that we were waiting for our taxis, in front of the stage door, on the sidewalk full of the city smells with some wet dog hair added for good measure. At that moment, Mary insisted on pulling me aside to tell something of importance.

"About Joanna," Mary said without any further ado, Maurice looming in the shadows, making sure we were getting in our cabs.

"So? Tell me!" I said.

She lowered her voice.

"They found a cloakroom stub for Brighton railway station."

"How is that relevant?" I asked, disappointed.

"Mortimer said they were excited about it."

"Men easily get excited. I wouldn't say that means anything."

"Mortimer explained."

"All right, tell me! Stop making me beg for it."

"But you like that, I thought."

"How do you know that?" I laughed.

"Sometimes, when you're late coming out of the dressing room, he waits for you. We talked a few times."

"About me?" I said, feeling the first pangs of jealousy. Mary was rather lovely, in a provincial, innocent sort of way.

She smiled apologetically.

"About the things I like?" I said, a fist slowly closing around my heart.

"Only a little," she said, "in jest."

I said nothing, staring at the tip of my umbrella, making ripples in the puddle by the sidewalk's edge.

"I am sorry, Lucy. I didn't mean anything by it. We were just talking."

"About what I like in bed!" I said, before remembering that Maurice was still nearby. I whispered, "I hope you had a good laugh."

"It wasn't like that. Honestly, Luce. We were passing the time!"

I looked at her face and saw tears silently rolling down her cheeks. I could tell she was looking at me like the little girl she had been, looking at the person taking her mother away to the asylum. I decided she meant what she said and that her heart, body and soul were the property of God.

And Constable Cooper.

I smiled and her tears ceased. I took out a handkerchief and questioned her while I dabbed her face.

"So, what was so important about that bloody stub?"

"For one thing," Mary started without missing a beat, happy to get the gossip off her chest and move on with her narrative, "Joanna had never been to Brighton."

"Could it have belonged to one of the previous tenants?"

"I asked exactly that!" Mary almost laughed. "Mortimer said that the apartment was thoroughly cleaned after each tenant, according to the landlady. Plus, the stub was found in the middle of the room, where Joanna would surely have found it. And a similar ticket was discovered nearby."

"Where? At Brighton Railway Station?" I asked, a little bored.

"No," Mary said mysteriously, "next to another murdered girl, in digs at Clapham."

"You're joking?" I stammered once I got my breath back. "In Clapham? That's miles away!"

"I know," Mary said, and her expression altered. "It seems the police are considering the two murders to be linked."

"Do you think?" I said, sarcastically.

"And they're now looking into other cases, to see whether stubs from Brighton were found."

"That seems unlikely. Unless the murderer is leaving us some kind of signature."

"Signature?"

"Yes. You see, some of them…"

But my taxicab arrived and the present got a lot more pressing than police investigative theories. I gave my companion a peck on the cheek and boarded my noisy chariot.

"Scotland Yard," I called over the engine racket.

"You in trouble, miss?" the driver asked through the open window.

"Not yet," I whispered as we sped away.

I reclined smiling as the night time streets and late strollers flew by my window. I must have dozed off because I woke with a start. He slammed on the anchors and the car abruptly stopped at Victoria Embankment.

"Thank you," I said, dropping a few shillings in the man's open palm.

I checked my coat and hat, my umbrella's handle hooked on my forearm. I made my way to the imposing double doors, very glad to be entering them by my own free will. Ever since January, I had kept the promise I made myself to stay out of trouble, at least the kind of trouble that would have brought me here escorted by a couple of bobbies.

The entrance hall was eerily quiet and surprisingly under lit. The high ceiling and wrought iron chandelier were barely visible. The brightest spot in the room was the lamp of the only manned desk.

With steps echoing noisily, my heels clicking on the black and white marble floor, I went over to the bobby at the registry desk. He slowly looked up from whatever papers he had been reading with such concentration. He seemed downright reluctant to engage in conversation with me. I supposed that, since I had entered with such poise and calm, he wasn't alarmed and assumed that nothing was amiss. Nonetheless, he came closer to the high counter as I smiled at him.

"How can I help you, miss?" he inquired.

'You can drop the condescending 'miss' for one thing,' I thought, but bit my tongue.

"I am here to report a break in," I said, still smiling.

"Of course," he said, pulling out a form from under the counter. I imagined a whole host of papers lying in earnest expectation of use beneath the counter.

"Let me fill out this form."

"Actually," I cooed, in my most delicate tone, "I was hoping to talk to an inspector."

"We only call upon inspectors if there is really something to investigate," he said, making me feel like I was eight years old.

"There's plenty to investigate, Constable...?"

"Barnes, Constable Barnes," he said, smiling kindly, taking the bait. "And what's so mysterious about your affair, miss?"

"Well," I started, doing my best to blush. "I'd prefer to talk about it with an inspector."

"You're going to have to do better than that, miss. I can't go calling on the nightshift inspector whenever a pretty little thing like you comes calling, can I, now?

"Really?" I smiled and rocked my body from side to side, like the naughty little girl I am. "What does one *have* to do?"

He delayed a few seconds. I guessed that my suggestion had fired his imagination, and probably other things, too.

"Why don't you tell me a little more about it and we'll see," he said leaning a little further forward.

"The thing is, Constable Barnes," I said, almost able to whisper into his ear, "I have some more information about the death of Joanna St John. I was her neighbour, you see."

"What?" he exclaimed, standing abruptly and looking at me as if I had just confessed to the deed itself. "We questioned all the neighbours."

"Not all of them, apparently," I said, smiling pleasantly. "I just came back from the country, with a friend, in Eastbourne."

"I see," he said, calming down somewhat.

"I'll fetch the inspector."

"Thank you," I said pursing my lips a little too much. But he was a like a hound on a fresh new scent and made off without turning round.

I was left to my own devices, in an echoing great hall. I had a look around, on tiptoe, the dimmed lights revealing great white walls and high, black rimmed windows. Left and right of the double doors was a long counter, about shoulder height, so constables could look down on the visitors. I was walking about as silently as I could and heard two constables in a back room, evidently playing cards. The back of the hall was open to the large stairwell, much wider than the one leading to the cells. Corridors plunged in darkness went off to the left and to the right in front of the stairs.

The perfect setting for my little trap.

I had seen a few lit windows upstairs from the outside so I assumed that more members of the police force were part of a night shift there. But they would not interfere with my plans. I hoped. They could be so contrary sometimes.

Much to my disappointment, Constable Barnes came down the darkened stairs alone, his step still hurried. He didn't bother to seek the refuge of his counter and came straight towards me. I welcomed him with a smile.

"Miss, if you'll follow me, please," he said sternly.

"And where are we going?" I asked, standing as still as I could, commanding confidence.

"The inspector is waiting for you in one of the upstairs interview rooms."

Not where they interrogated suspects. Good.

"And which inspector will I be talking to?" I asked.

"What's it to you?" he snapped. "He'll take your statement, that's what you want, isn't it?"

"Yes, constable," I answered, like the good girl I was not.

Gruffly, he hurried up the stairs and down the corridor to the left. He opened the door to the first interview room on the left, the only one with lights on. As I turned onto the doorstep, I saw him, sitting there, his gold brown locks lit by the bare light bulb, his blue eyes ready to appraise the impudent late night visitor. He really had no inkling! It was a relief and a pleasure to see his broad smile of surprise.

"The lady who asked to see you, inspector," Barnes said.

His tone led me to think he may not have been as gullible as I first thought. All the same, I stepped into the room and sat down, across from the inspector.

"Thank you, Barnes," the inspector said in his offhand way, looking at me. "Please close the door."

The constable looked at each of us in turn like an evil headmaster and left, demonstratively closing the door.

"Now that's what I call a bad idea," Inspector Cumberland said.

"Oh come on!" I purred, putting my hand on his. "Don't tell me you're not even a little pleased to see me."

"A little. And apprehensive. How did you get Barnes to show you up here?"

"I told him I was Joanna's neighbour," I said proudly.

"And?"

"That I had information about her death."

"Do you?"

"None that I haven't heard form Mary, who heard it from her constable sweetheart."

"I see," Barney said thoughtfully. "Which one is it, again?"

"You're not going to get him into trouble, are you?"

"I would never!" he said, piqued.

"His name is Mortimer Cooper. His beat is in our neighbourhood."

"How romantic."

"What would you know about romance?"

"True," he said, "which brings us to our next topic. What *are* you doing here?"

"I only wanted to see you," said Lucy, the little girl.

"I see," he said, aware of my playfulness.

"And I knew your chief was miffed enough to have you on a nightshift three times in a row."

"That's awfully thoughtful of you," he said, taking my hand.

"I thought you might be in need of some… distraction."

"I knew there was a primary motive."

"Oh absolutely," I said, kissing his fingers. "If you want me to leave, just say so," I said, putting his hand down on the table.

"No," he said, squeezing my hand gently. "Please stay."

I will not deny that my heart fluttered a little when I heard him say that, and the hoarseness of his voice turned me on. I gazed at him and squeezed his hand. For a moment, we managed to look only at each other, our heart beats deafening in the silent police station. I suppose it looked dreadfully amorous, and I'll admit that breathing became a little more difficult. Yes, I did have a motive to show up that night. I congratulated myself for having made it that far.

"And now, Miss Hall, what would you have us do?"

Slowly, my eyes on his, I guided his hand into the depths of my décolletage, beneath my half opened coat and dress. After a moment, that hand found its way around by itself and I could let go. He stared at me intently.

"And how do you propose we do this?" he said, still busy with rearranging the contents of my brassiere.

"I thought you might have somewhere private you could interrogate me undisturbed," I said, my eyes half shut.

"That can be arranged," he said, slowly withdrawing his hand.

He stood, slow and deliberate. First, he pulled me close and kissed me hard. Every time, it surprised me. How could so much passion be so well concealed behind such a cool façade? I was usually agreeably surprised by his kisses. I constantly had to question who had more desire for the other, a most amusing game. In the last six months, I had convinced myself that I had to make him tag along. But, when it got down to business, he was just as keen as me.

He pulled me towards the door and switched off the light. We were now standing in the darkened interview room, his hand in mine. The light from the occupied desks down the hall threw a milky pallor though the frosted glass in the door. He slowly pushed down the door handle and managed to open it soundlessly. We had to make a left down the corridor and walked all the way around the door, silently.

Once safe, he took my hand and we ventured further into darkness, leaving the lit office hall behind us. We walked on tiptoe. With one hand, he felt his way along the wall, door after door, seeking one in particular. The other hand was securely around my waist, slowly making its way south. I hoped the room he sought was going to show up soon. My body was yearning for this encounter, his cheeky hand only firing me on.

Just as I was about to make him trip and initiate matters on the cold black and white floor, he stopped. A door opened next to me, a pitch-black room behind it. I felt his hand pushing me inside and heard the door close. For the briefest moment, I let myself be frightened and pretended I wasn't with the kindest, politest and most exciting, excited, man in Scotland Yard.

I didn't know where I was. There was absolutely no light, no window, no airshaft, nothing. As he kissed and pushed me against a table, I smelt cleaning products and heard the clang of glass and metal containers.

We really had made it into the proverbial broom closet. Quaint.

There was nothing quaint about what was to happen in that closet. Just as he kept kissing me, he lifted me onto the table and started undoing my coat and shirt. I missed the light. He was so beautiful in those moments with his blue eyes turning almost purple and his flushed cheeks. I could feel his breath on my bare shoulders and back as he kissed my neck. Shudders covered my skin and I started moaning under my breath. His right hand travelled along my thigh, pushing my skirt up in the process.

Since I had counted on our encounter taking such a turn, I had left my knickers in my purse, hoping there would be no gusts of wind on my journey to the police station. Barney's agile hand found its way to my slit and pearl and started teasing with his middle finger. Spasms of pleasure ran up and down my body. With his left hand, he pressed my lips to his, his body in tune with my seizures of pleasure.

When the first round of my ecstasy culminated, I helped release him. We had become quite oblivious of the rest of the world, not even remembering to tone down our own noise. We roared, we sighed, we cried. The rush of desire, the drunkenness of the senses, the joy of togetherness overcame any consequence in the real, dull world beyond the door.

The storm we whipped up grew violent, and like a failed quest for the stars, our journey ended in an explosion of a thousand luminescent fires.

We stayed immobile and silent for a little while, as close as any two human beings could ever be. I felt his lips on mine, a parting kiss, prelude to our silent coming apart.

I was about to open the door to check whether our brief encounter had attracted anybody's attention when he grabbed my arm and pulled me close. I turned to face him. He was wearing his jacket and belt again, I could tell, even in the encompassing darkness. He gently pulled my face to his and kissed me again, softly, sincerely. Then he took me in his arms and hugged me. For a moment, I was terrified that this was his way of saying goodbye, but he whispered a few words and all my fears melted like snow in early Spring.

I suppose regular girls want to hear those words from the man they're sweet on, especially after they've shared such moments, but for a dancing girl, it's often the overture to relinquish her principles for any random punter. When I heard Barney whispering them to me, first I was relieved, wanting to believe them so much. Next, I was frightened. Barnaby was no stranger to the world I inhabited. He knew how many times a girl in my line of work would hear them when they meant nothing. So why would he say them to me? We didn't need them. We didn't need conventions or commonplace declarations of love. Was I being unfair? Barney probably meant them because he knew my life and because he knew I heard them too often when they had meant nothing. I had heard them many a time from an intoxicated customer, but also, more desperately, from my mother, before being taken to a 'rest home', never to leave. Barnaby had probably wanted me to hear them because he knew I needed them. How he knew is a mystery to me, but I loved him for it.

Unable to give him a spontaneous and sincere answer in the middle of my turmoil, I responded by kissing him again. And again. Maybe also to keep him from saying anything else.

He stepped in front of me and took my hand, silently pulling me along the dark side of the corridor until we reached the stairwell and the lit rows of desks. Swiftly we made our way downstairs. On the landing between floors, where neither the front desk nor the upstairs employees could see us, we kissed one last time. He gave me that warm, all forgiving, sublime smile and climbed back upstairs. I walked through the entrance hall, deaf to whatever Constable Barnes said to me.

It was only when I stood on the sidewalk, waiting for a cab, the wind blowing in my face announcing the next rainstorm, that the same words slipped from my lips, carried away by the gust. "Me too," I murmured. "I love you."

Due to the preceding night's encounter, I slept quite late and showed up just in time for the afternoon rehearsal. The dressing room was heaving with gossip and laughter, the girls all being in a jolly mood. Upon first bells, we made our way upstairs.

Mrs Bartlett was waiting for us with a long face. Was she jealous of our merriment or had she had a bad morning? No one knew, but she was even more unforgiving than usual. Mary had been making eyes at me all the while, so at the first water break, I went over to her. I wondered if she knew anything and if Mrs Bartlett's mood had anything to do with Joanna's inquiry.

When I joined Mary, I saw that all the kindness had vanished from her face. She was all nerves, wringing her hands, her eyes darting, her breath short. She practically dragged me into a dark corner of the wings. It was a risky move because we weren't that numerous and Mrs Bartlett would no doubt start her rehearsal again soon, noticing our absence in a matter of seconds, but my friend's dismay was so apparent that I willingly took that risk.

I had grown quite fond of her over the past six months, taking her on the occasional shopping spree or out dancing. I wondered if anything had happened to her boyfriend, Constable Cooper. It was the only reason I could think of to make a sensible girl like Mary lose her composure like that.

"Lucy, you have to help me," Mary whispered.

"Of course, Mary. What is it?"

Her eyes flicked round as if spies were lurking in the shadows. Apparently, what she saw did not satisfy her because she pulled me even further into the backstage area, right next to the tabs store and the stage loading door.

"It's my cousin, James Armstrong."

"You have a cousin? I didn't know that."

"He will be arrested tomorrow," she interrupted.

"Why?"

"I can't tell you. Luce, but we have to go there, tonight!"

"Go where, Mary?"

"To Shadwell."

"Shadwell? I am not going anywhere near Shadwell, especially at night, Mary! Don't you know how dangerous it is down by the docks? Anyway, I am wearing my white gloves dress. I am meeting someone after the show."

"Lucy! You have to help us! James will be waiting at the train station. He will walk with us all the time."

"What on Earth would we want to do in Shadwell? Surely your cousin can take care of himself. He doesn't need us."

"He can take care of himself, but he's not too bright. He needs someone to help him think things through and make the right decision."

"Whether or not to run from the police? I recommend not to try," I said by way of conclusion, getting ready to return to our rehearsal. Mrs Bartlett was already calling our names. Mary caught me by the arm.

"It's more complicated than that, Lucy. He's told the coppers too much and now he's going to be arrested or killed by one of his own."

"Alright, fine," I said, giving way, tempted by the challenge of keeping a good man out of prison, maybe even saving his life, and taking on the idiots, bar one, at Scotland Yard. "I'll go with you. Now let's go back to work."

Mary repeated a thousand thank yous as she followed me to the stage. Of course, Mrs Bartlett gave us a good going over. I took the brunt of it, as best I could, protecting Mary. We fell in line and joined the others in the warm up exercises.

That's when I noticed the girl who had been hired to replace Rachel.

Sometimes I had the impression Mrs Huff had a stash of new girls hidden away and pulled one out whenever she needed them. What a ghastly image! Mrs Huff as our very own Bluebeard!

The girl in question, Flora Murdoch, was the very opposite of Rachel, blonde, blue eyed, thin limbed, angelic innocence written all over her face, the softest voice and the most graceful poise. Had I been so inclined, I would've liked to get to know her better. 'Much better,' as our gentlemen liked to say when they bought us champagne after the show. But I doubted her and did not like her. I knew her type too well. She may have looked different from Rachel, but I would bet my last farthing that her soul, hidden behind that adorable façade, was far darker than

Rachel's.

So there I was, "*tendu*, close, *tendu*," having met my nemesis. It may sound overly dramatic but something told me that the girl was trouble. By that, I mean she would instinctively know I was something of a leader in our little mêlée and would seek to tear that crown from my head. She might even go after Barney. I am as modest in my own way, but I must say that he is rather dashing.

It was with an unfamiliar knot in my stomach that I let Mrs Bartlett push me around to find the proper position for Mrs Huff's next vision. The more I watched Flora, giggling with her new found friends, modestly putting her hand in front of her mouth, the more my features hardened and my heart shrank. She was a gifted dancer too, taking direction seamlessly, altering her pause, the beat of her steps and the position of her arms obediently. I could tell that Mrs Bartlett was thoroughly taken by her. There goes her first victim. And the girls were not far behind, none of them having her classical training.

When that dreadful rehearsal finally came to an end, I dragged myself downstairs, pretending to be tired by the lengthy bout on stage. We had a light dinner of sandwiches and champagne, sent by one of Ethel's and Greta's admirers. And then, the show started.

The red and white lollipops twirled, the kimonos shimmered gracefully in the subdued 'opium den'-like lighting, the kilts flew high in the air with every step we took. Everything was *'calme, luxe et volupté'* on the deck of our cruise ship and the audience nearly broke furniture at the end of the tap dance routine. Throughout, Flora was perfect, as if she had never done any other show. The bits of conversation I overheard let me know that the girls were, as I had predicted, impressed by her skills and quite happy with her demeanour in the dressing room.

As a matter of habit, Rachel's table had been taken over by Norma, who was now next to me, the stage stairs separating us, and Tina, Greta and Bridget had budged down one table. Hence, Flora was next to Mary at the far end of the dressing room. She was far enough from me to afford a little peace of mind.

We were all chatting and getting dressed after the show, some to meet the audience, some to go home to their beau or their fiancé. I slowly took off my stage make up, subdued. It was unlike me but no one seemed to notice until the voice of my genie sounded right next to me.

"Lucy," Mary said, pressing, but in whispers, "what are you doing? We have to go! My cousin is waiting for us. His life may be in danger!"

I had quite forgotten about Mary's cousin's predicament. I found myself needing to do this, to see her cousin in one of the few places in London where even I shivered at the thought of being alone, indeed, of what would happen if any girl was left alone.

I enjoy a challenge and I embraced adventure in all its forms. So, in a matter of minutes, I was amongst the first ones to be ready to leave. One may think me easily distracted but there is nothing like a whiff of danger to get me out of my gloom. Arm in arm, Mary and I walked to Charing Cross station and took the District Line, then the Metropolitan to Shadwell.

As we got off, I was struck by two things. First, the smell and the appearance of the buildings was worse than I had expected. Second, the idea of visiting the docks at night seemed like a spectacularly bad idea.

I was lot more frightened than I had expected. I suggested as much to Mary, as quietly as I could, so as to not give any of the dockside workers and assorted sailors around us any bad ideas. She shrugged and calmly walked over to one of the larger, taller and cleaner men standing about.

For a change, I was entirely out of my depth, so I followed her dutifully. She was quieter than usual and I knew it should have worried me, but quite the contrary was true. I was excited that so serious a matter would be brought before me. And in such an unlikely place.

The man she spoke to was her cousin James Armstrong. Behind the rough exterior, he was quite charming and polite. Looking all about, he said, "Pigster's death has made everybody nervous. We should go home."

With that, he put his large hands on our shoulders and guided us towards his destination.

He walked a slow walk, tipping from side to side as if he wasn't on land at all. He led us through a barely lit backstreet, full of stray cats and rotting waste. Mary was walking by his side, apparently unaware of the squalor around. Every now and then, she looked up with touching affection at her mysterious cousin.

I was unable to relax, feeling the dirt around

us becoming contagious. I started wondering how close these cousins really were. I hadn't known Mary that long, but she had never mentioned him.

Not long after, James stopped in front of one of the many doors lining the narrow street, homes of the men of the sea. He produced a key that looked minute in his large hands and opened the door for us. Mary, very much at home, walked into the common room to our right and told me to sit while she headed into the kitchen to put on the kettle. James vanished silently upstairs.

I tried to cope with my surroundings but I had become unaccustomed to that degree of poverty. I didn't know whether the worn chair would hold me nor how flea infested was the ancient, tattered cushion.

I had fallen on bad times myself but somehow, even at the worst of times, I was able to find refuge in places nicer than this. They might have included some plump gentleman who had to be entertained every so often, but how else is a teenager to stay off the streets? The 1920s may have been roaring for the rich and famous, but for me they were years of survival, one way or the other.

Back in Shadwell, I took in the common room. Its wilted dark green wallpaper and cheap furniture were the décor of the room where the men living upstairs gathered for breakfast and tea, meaning the evening meal. The wooden floor was dusty and had not seen lacquer in some time. A gas chandelier, its chrome in bad need of polishing, hung in the middle of the room, its six grimy glass shades casting a semblance of light.

I was still coping with all of this when Mary and James returned. He had changed his shirt and washed his face. She was carrying a tea tray with a pot, three non-matching cups and saucers and stale biscuits. Smiling at my apparent dismay, they sat down on either side of me, at the large bare table.

Since they arrived together, I was unable to question Mary about the relationship with her cousin, but I made a note to ask her later. As she started pouring the tea, James crossed his large hands on the table and turned his amicable face towards me, his eyes looking intently at mine.

"So," he started in his baritone voice, "What has Mary told you?"

"Nothing," I stammered, befuddled by his big brown eyes.

"Good," he continued, looking over my shoulder at his smiling cousin. "The thing is, you see, Miss…?"

"Please, call me Lucy."

"The thing is, Miss Lucy, I told the coppers too much and now I am a suspect and they're comin' to arrest me, very soon, in the mornin', so the tip-off says."

"I am sorry," I replied, "but you will have to start from the beginning. What did you tell the police?" I asked.

"She really hasn't told you a thing?" he said, looking at her, leaning forward a little.

"No! I didn't want to get her mixed up in this. I know how much you want to help, Luce, but when James told me the coppers were coming for him, I was desperate. We needed help."

"*We* needed help. How she is!" he said, beaming at his cousin. "The story is, Miss Lucy, that two days ago someone found the body of one of my friends. Pigster was his name. They found him in a rubbish heap not far from here and I know who did it. But the coppers are blaming me."

"How are you a suspect?" I asked.

"Because the coppers don't have a brain between them, even if you count the whole squad. I saw everythin' so I must've done it, they reckon. And the other lads at the shipyard don't like a squealer. So they made it sound like I was the one. That's all the coppers wanted to hear."

"And you know who the killer is?" I said, my curiosity definitely piqued.

"'Course I do! I saw'em just as I see you. Tiggy and Moosh! Pushin' poor Pigster around, they were! They didn't like Pigster too much. He had found half a loaf of bread, he had."

"A loaf of bread?" I asked. "No one kills for a loaf of bread."

"These lads did. As I said, they didn't like the look of pour ol' Pigster. Maybe Tiggy and Moosh were hungry or lookin' for trouble. I don't know for sure, but they gave Pigster a good thrashing and shoved him on the rubbish heap. I couldn't let them get away with it, so right or wrong, I went and told the coppers."

It was a story of roughnecks, anger, violence and no little mystery. Just up my street.

"How can I help?" I asked.

The two cousins exchanged such an agreeing glance that I was thrilled and terrified, all at once.

"That's a good question," he said, feeding me my rope. "They say that Pigster was killed by someone hittin' him with a blunt instrument to the back of the head. Now I saw Tiggy walking around with an axe, like he was out to do harm. I saw it clear as day. And yesterday, I found that same axe in the back garden of this house - my house, that is - with dark stuff stuck to the lug. Blood, dried blood. Ready for the coppers to find. Like I had something to do with it. I didn't. Nothing at all. That axe was planted, Miss, planted."

I did not say anything, but listened intently. There must have been a smile on my face because James said, "I don't know why you're smilin', Miss! I don't know what to do! If they find it here, I am goin' to hang!"

"That's where you come in," Mary said, putting a hand on my shoulder and patting my back.

"Where do I come in? I don't see."

"Mary says you're awful clever, and brave, and you know coppers."

"One in particular who just happens to work this part of town?"

Mary smiled and winked at me.

"While that may all be true," I said, giving Mary a 'shut up' glance, "I still don't see, how I'm supposed to help you?"

I was wringing the life out of the white gloves I'd taken off as I walked in. James and Mary were looking at me with so much hope, like two children at story time on Christmas Eve.

"You are smart, Lucy," Mary said, very serious. "Help us make this go away."

"Now really," I started, "I don't see what I could possibly…"

And it came to me. The answer, plain and simple. Like a telegram inside my head.

"Someone should hide the axe at Tiggy's and Moosh's."

Just enough rope to hang yourself, as they say.

They looked at each other, flabbergasted, then stared at me, their mouths practically gaping. I was uncertain whether that momentary lapse of reaction was their expression of admiration or loss at the madness of my idea. In an attempt to jolt them back to life, I asked them a simple question.

"Are they working tonight? Maybe we should do it before the police shows up."

"And who's goin' to do it?" James mumbled, still staring at me as if I was a three horned elk.

"Well, you can't be seen near their shack, so maybe I could go, and Mary could be on the lookout."

"Oh, no, Lucy. I came with you to that chess player's house, but that was before I knew what you intended to do. I am not brave like you. Please, don't ask me!"

"I can't go in there alone, Mary. For one thing, I don't know where it is. And for another, there are dangerous chaps out there."

"That's exactly why I am not going."

"Mary," James intervened calmly. "I could follow from afar. I could stay in the shadows and make sure you both are safe."

"Really, Jimmy, you think that's a good idea?"

I had never met anyone actually called Jimmy before so I tried to assimilate that information. Meanwhile, the two cousins carried on their argument about whether or not we were going to hide the axe at Tiggy's and

Moosh's. Since I knew it was the best option, I was quite happy to blank out for a bit. When they noticed the absent look on my face, Mary shook me by the arm.

"So?" I said, as if I had woken from a pleasant nap. "Are we going?"

"Yes," replied Mary, somewhat less than enthusiastically.

"And I'll be close by, watching." James said with a surprising flair for the dramatic.

"Good," I said as if we were going punting on the Serpentine. "Let's go."

I put on my gloves and hat. James helped Mary into her coat. We walked out of the door into the dim street. It was as uncongenial and clammy as before.

"So, where is this bloody thing?"

"Lucy!" Mary scolded me, quite shocked.

"Sorry, I didn't mean it like that. I meant to say, James, would you be so kind as to hand me the item we need to be rid of?"

"Sure, Miss, I'll fetch it from the back."

He disappeared into the ink black night between the two buildings.

Mary and I stood close to each other, in that under-lit street, listening to the noises of the night, men and women shouting, loving, babies crying, cats fighting, dogs barking, the boats whistling on the docks, the cranes creaking under their heavy load. Somewhere, at the back of my mind, I realized that an idea could seem perfectly sound in a warmly lit parlour but lose its shine every step closer to realisation.

James emerged from the shadows before my doubts could turn into proper concern.

I took the parcel he gave me, not particularly worried about how well the strings had been tied around the brown wrapping paper.

"Lead the way," I said, encouragingly.

He pointed in the direction of an even more ghastly décor than the one we had just left. I acted as if it was a lovely day in May and hurried on, my arm hooked under Mary's. She tried to keep up, truly frightened by the neighbourhood. I could vaguely hear James' footsteps a few feet behind us.

"So, tell me, what's between you and 'Jimmy'?" I asked, low enough to make sure he wouldn't hear us.

"What?" Mary whispered. "He's my cousin! What are you talking about?"

"I understand, but…"

"No! Listen, Luce, I don't how things were done in your family, but we are cousins, that's it."

"Leave my family out of it. You don't want to know how weird things can be with posh folk. You seem to like him, a lot."

"Yes, he's adorable, the nicest man you'll ever meet, and he's always there to help me when I need him. I had to get him the best help I could."

"If you're from Dundee and he's a docker in Shadwell, how come you two are this close?"

"I moved to Dundee two years ago, for a maid's position in a family. Before that, we lived in the same house in Stepney."

"I see," I said, feeling that she wasn't telling me the whole story.

"He took care of my mother, Mrs Huff's sister, and of me, when she died," she said, as if reading my thoughts.

"Took care of you?" I purred.

"Lucy, I am eighteen. I did a lot of growing up in Dundee. When we lived in the family house, I was protected and he kept it that way."

"Good for you," I said, strangely disappointed at the sweetness and light of the story's conclusion.

We had meandered in Shadwell for a little over ten minutes and reached the railway bridge. Under each arch, all manner of dwellings and workshops had been erected. Even in the dark, the indigent lives of these people bothered me.

Something else bothered me, too.

I turned around, speaking blindly into the night.

"James, what if they're home?"

It was a blindingly obvious question that needed an answer.

"They're still at the pub, drinking today's wages."

I had no option but to believe him. Mary, though, pulled me back, nervous.

"I have a bad feeling about this, Luce."

"And yet you want me to help. Any better ideas?"

She had none.

"It's a bit like visiting cavemen," I said, in jest. "Don't fret, Mary. You heard the man, they aren't home."

"They could come back any minute."

"As long as there's ale, money and music, why would they possibly want to return to this?"

"All right," Mary sighed. "Let's be quick about it."

"That's my girl. James, which one is it?"

"The fourth one down," came his growling whisper out of the shadows between two warehouses. "The one with two shacks and a large barrel between the two doors."

"Alright. I see. Let's go, Mary."

We walked down the paved alley, prudently but with enough momentum to look like we belonged there. Any sailors or dockers we met, we made no eye contact with and they left us alone. The moon was covered by thick rain clouds and from afar we could hear the boats and life around them. I felt a tremor of fear as I made my decision, but I had come this far and wasn't the kind of girl to walk on by.

The arch to our left was the one we were looking for. Dropping the contents of the parcel in there meant not only that James was going to stay out of jail but that two probably very unsavoury characters were going to hang. I took a deep breath, let go of Mary's arm and plunged into the pungent cesspool that was one of these men's home.

In the twilight, I could just make out a

rudimentary bed with a coarse wool blanket thrown open to shamelessly reveal the bed sheets that, even in this light, were clearly foul. Next to the bed stood an upturned crate of wine bottles with an oil lamp. Against the far wall was an old wardrobe with both doors missing. In it hung, surprisingly neat, all the man's clothes. The floor was strewn with half opened boxes and packages, fallen off some boat, no doubt. Dirty rags and blankets finished off the bounty I had stumbled upon.

By the time I had taken it all in, I stood in front of the trunk with every intention of simply dropping the axe in it, hiding it a little and be gone. Unfortunately, I now remembered that the parcel was not only wrapped in brown paper but also tied up with string. The wrapping would have made a postman proud but was a thorough nuisance to me. How foolish for not thinking this through beforehand!

Being without a penknife or a pair of scissors, I had to remove my gloves and undo the knots. As luck would have it, I heard from far away the noise of drunken men approaching. The chances were that one or both of our boys would be amongst them.

Mary was urging me to hurry. That did not help to steady my hand. In one last desperate attempt, I pulled on the string and managed to loosen one end enough to thread the whole thing out. The axe came free. Holding it with the paper, I carefully laid it out at the bottom of the trunk and pulled a worn woolly jumper over it.

Success!

Which was when I noticed that one of my gloves was missing.

As I looked around for it, Mary's voice sounded, closer and more urgent.

"Lucy," she whispered, "we have to leave now!"

The approaching songs and laughter told me as much. Renouncing the glove, I ran out and grabbed Mary's arm, aiming straight to the shadowy spot where James stood waiting. We ran straight into his arms. He put his hands over our mouths and we silently watched on, there in the dark recess smelling of cat's urine.

Tiggy and Moosh and two other ruffians came stumbling into view. They bade each other good night in the coarsest terms and vanished into their dwellings. I had expected one of them to discover the axe right away and come running out in fury but, after a few minutes of silence, which seemed like hours to me and my terrified heart, the only sound we heard were snores.

We waited another few minutes before silently making our way back to James' house.

Mary and James wanted to walk me to the station but, emboldened by the adventure, I told them I could take care of myself, that everyone was asleep and that the station wasn't far. After heartfelt goodbyes in which James insisted I saved his life, I walked towards the station, along the same dingy streets as before.

Maybe my anxiety was playing tricks on me but the silence on the way back seemed more intense than on the way there. I know I had company at the time but it had seemed more alive somehow. I dismissed the thought with a shrug and walked resolutely on.

These sensations should have whispered some warning in my ear. Maybe they did and I ignored them. I was too busy congratulating myself for a job well done and my courage under pressure.

Which was when I felt a pair of hands close around my throat and pull me down a flight of cellar steps.

I was pulled inside a pitch black space. One of the hands around my neck released me for a moment to partially close a door. My perpetrator didn't seem to mind as he pushed me down on my back.

With one hand, he lifted my skirt and busied himself with his belt buckle with the other. He sat on me to hold me down while I wriggled.

I started screaming, a somewhat foolish attempt as the odds of my cries being heard by someone willing and able to help were slim at best. The assailant put his coarse hand over my mouth, his knees holding my arms to my side. I realised that I could only count on myself to get out of that predicament.

I breathed slow and silent. He interpreted this as resilience and hurried up. I gathered my thoughts and planned my defence. I was older and stronger now. I was going to defend myself this time.

"She's not makin' a fuss anymore, ain't she?" said the toothless drunk tramp on top of me, breathing heavily in my face.

I had little time to act, so I had to act precisely. He had managed to remove his belt but seemed quite clueless as to how to remove his pants or get himself into position without letting go of my arms or mouth. He didn't seem to have a weapon or he surely would have threatened me with it, but the possibility of knocking me out was fast approaching, I could tell.

I took a deep breath and raised my upper body into a near sitting position, sharp, fast and furious. The sudden movment surprised the scoundrel and he fell on his back. Free to move, I jumped to my feet and stood by his waist.

"This is so you never do that again," I hissed.

With my not particularly high heel, I brought my foot down on his groin.

A horrid wail pierced the night as he bent forward and away from me.

I didn't wait to hear the litany of insults that came pouring out of his mouth, as freely as the blood pouring on the coal dust covered floor. I dashed out into the street as fast as I could.

As the cool of the night met me, I started trembling all over, my nerves entirely frayed.

I looked around. Thankfully, two bobbies were standing beneath a lamp at the end of the street. I approached them, still shaking.

They were worried about my distressed and

dishevelled appearance. I told them where to find the thug and that I would be fine if they would just find me a cab. Somehow, through all this, I had kept a hold of my purse.

Which is more than can be said of my peace of mind.

And one white glove.

I slept uncomfortably that night, bumps, bruises and strains making themselves progressively known all over my body. No doubt, foundation would have to be spread on a little thicker and on rather unusual places for the show. I was concordantly late for my luncheon appointment with Barnaby. I wish I could say I was running late but all I could do was walk, and painfully slow at that.

My left ankle had violently bumped against the doorframe as I was dragged downstairs. I managed to keep the swelling to a minimum with lavender oil but it forbade any kind of running. Hence, I casually walked into the Coal Hole Pub a good thirty minutes late.

It was the kind of place I ended up going to regularly. Somehow, it felt like home. We used to regularly change our lunch meeting venue so as to not attract attention, but of late it hadn't seemed so important. I noticed him standing on the mezzanine, at the back. I could feel his angry blue eyes burning into the top of my head as I walked up to the counter, greeting the bartender with a cheerful, "Hello George!" and ordering lunch for two. I briefly looked up and smiled at him as if everything was all right. I walked up the stairs as elegantly as I could, my legs failing and my half pint feeling almost too heavy to hold.

As soon as we were alone, I let some of my exhaustion show. Instead of giving me a hard time, which he had probably been chewing on for some time, Barney rushed over.

"Darling, what's going on?" he said as he made me sit down, putting my half pint next to his on the table.

"I had a rather eventful night."

"Isn't that the norm in your line of work?" he asked as he pecked me on the cheek, right on the spot where the lout's hand had held me down so hard, my cheek had turned black and blue. I winced. "Darling! Tell me what's going on?"

"Would you horribly mind if I didn't tell you? I don't want you to be worried."

"I'll only be worried if you don't tell me," he said sternly. I understood why criminals were afraid of him.

"It's nothing. A little too much champagne."

"All right," he said, looking at me suspiciously, letting go of my hands. "Any reason why are you wearing so much make up?"

It was a particularly sunny day in June and even here, at the top of the mezzanine, at the back of a pub, the thick layer of foundation was evident. It was a lot more than I usually wore, though less than I'd put on for the show. It didn't take much for an intuitive detective like him to catch on.

"It was nothing, darling, please, don't worry," I tried to appease him.

It didn't work. He kept staring at me as if I had stolen his mother's pearls. I sighed in defeat and rapidly sorted through the events so as to not let slip how much I was meddling in police business. I suppose I should have even lied about being in Shadwell but I was too tired to conjure up a convincing fib.

"I am sorry, darling. I didn't mean to lie to you," I said, contrite, which softened him a little. "I was visiting a friend in Shadwell, after the show."

"A friend? In Shadwell? What friend?"

His question had many implications. He might have been suggesting that I had gone back to my old ways. We had, after all, been 'seeing' each other for over six months, which was, he knew, a record for me. I had been faithful to him all that time, occasionally but professionally flirting with some of the patrons who had requested me by name at the theatre after the show. I felt quite vexed and some of the old fire rekindled in my eyes and cheeks.

"I went to see Mary's cousin, with her," I said angrily. "If you are going to doubt everything I say, Barney, I might as well leave."

"No, wait, I'm sorry," he said, catching my hand as I pretended to get up. "You know how jealous I get. That's why I never come to see your shows. I don't know what I would do if I sat next to one of those chaps shouting lewd things at you."

"You're so sweet," I said as I caressed his cheek and kissed him.

"But you shouldn't be in Shadwell at night, you know that."

"I know. It was an emergency," I said as I

took off my jacket. Rather stupidly I had forgotten that I was wearing a short-sleeved shirt. Barney jumped at the sight of the two nasty bruises on my forearms where the attacker's knees had pinned me down. He grabbed my wrists and lifted my arms to get a better look. He was angry and his gaze conveyed the extent to which he felt betrayed.

"Lucy," he said, his voice far too controlled. "What did you do? What have they done to you?"

"It's all right, Barnaby, really," I pleaded, trying to free my wrists from his grip. "It looks worse than it is, I promise."

"Fine," he said, kissing my wrists before laying them down in my lap. "Start talking."

I am quite sure that was the language he used with his prisoners but I didn't dwell on it. He was upset for all the right reasons and it was up to me to put his mind at ease.

"Please stop worrying. It was my fault. Well, I brought it upon myself. I was visiting Mary's cousin and decided to walk back to the station alone. It was quite late and they did offer to walk with me but I refused. You know how I can be, always independent. The station wasn't far at all and I was quite confident I could make it without incident. Unfortunately, I was wrong. A man grabbed me from behind and dragged me into a coal cellar."

The look of pain on Barnaby's face was clear.

"Don't worry, my sweet, I freed myself before anything untoward happened."

"'Anything untoward'? Lucy, you must be joking. What happened is terrible. You poor thing!"

"I know, but I am all right. Two policemen were nearby and put me in a cab. I was home in no time. I am fine."

"Look at your arms! You are not fine."

"Barnaby, stop mothering me. I am a big girl, used to sordid types. I have been taking care of myself for the past ten years. I was careless. Let's not make a fuss out of this, please."

He was reluctant to let it go, of course.

"Did you report it?" he asked.

"What?" I said, taken aback.

"Your attack, did you report it to the policemen?"

"I was too shaken up to think of it, to be honest."

"What were their names?" he said, pulling

out his trusted notepad from his coat pocket.

"What? I didn't notice, Barney. I was shaken up, I tell you."

"A minute ago, you told me it was nothing."

"A minute ago, I didn't want to worry you."

He put the notepad in his breast pocket and taking my hand tenderly said, "I can find out easily enough who was doing the rounds on that beat last night. How are you feeling now?"

"I am all right," I smiled, taking his hand in both of mine.

His face relaxed and he seemed to believe me. I was so happy to have him next to me now. I couldn't bear to see him worried about me. Despite his aloof manners and serious demeanour, I had seen his more sensitive side. We had been friends for two years and grown closer at the end of 1930. In spite of our very different backgrounds, we got along tremendously well. Our mingled hands, his warm smile upon me, the dull roar of lunchtime conversations in the pub below and the traffic on The Strand outside, I was basking under a warm blanket of comfort, far away from the dreadful event of the night before.

The moment was interrupted by George and

his two platters of lunch, bangers and mash. How romantic.

"Funny you should be in Shadwell last night," he said, chewing on a mouthful of delicious pub food. "I was in Shadwell this morning, carrying out an arrest."

He was making conversation, I hoped, but my heart was racing and I was holding my breath. I took a sip of my pint before starting on lunch. I looked down at my plate, thinking of James, to give me some kind of courage.

"Really?" I was as casual as I could be. "Who was it?"

"No one of importance, as you can imagine. Two thugs at the docks."

My mind raced. Two thugs. Not one.

"What did they do?"

"Murder apparently. They're linked to a dead body we found in a smouldering rubbish pile a few days ago."

"Why did you arrest them?"

"You're full of questions, today, aren't you?" he said, gently touching my cheek. "We arrested them because of an anonymous telephone call. Sure enough, we found the murder weapon at the bottom of a trunk in the suspects' yard."

"Didn't they protest innocence?" I asked, trying to appear a lot less interested than I was.

"One did. Those dockers have the most original nicknames, you know. The one they call Tiggy is actually Oliver Marks. He protested quite a bit. But when he said he had nothing to do with 'that tattooed fellow being done in', we asked him how he knew. He didn't reply, of course."

"And the other one?" I asked, again not too eagerly.

"I am answering your questions to humour you, Luce, and because I know you enjoy these stories but I should keep you from any excitement."

"Keep trying," I said, kissing him. "Why don't you put me to bed instead?"

"Not what I had in mind," he said surprised.

"I did."

"I know, but not what you need. Let me get on with the story," he said, pointing at the plate in front of me, which I had barely touched while his was almost empty.

"If you insist," I said, still hiding my desperate curiosity.

"The second fellow is quite a character. His

nickname is Moosh, real name is William Kelly. Disappointing, eh? But he isn't, let me tell you. He put up a fight and when they finally managed to put cuffs on him, he walked by me so proudly, for a moment, I actually doubted we had the right man."

"And do you?"

"What?"

"Have the right man? The right men?"

"Yes, I hope so. If the axe in the trunk isn't damning enough, there is always the testimony of the witness."

"There was a witness?"

I swallowed hard.

"Yes. Imagine that. Those two idiots attacked Herbert Ayles, better known as Pigster, in the street and someone saw them, another worker, a man named James Armstrong."

I didn't quite choke.

"Was he suspected of anything?"

"No, why?"

"I just find it convenient that you found the murder weapon in the shack of one of the two men this Armstrong fellow told you about."

"Unless they're guilty. But you are right, Luce. There are some disturbing details in this case."

The food was harder and harder to swallow.

"Like what?"

"One detail in particular. A glove."

"A glove?" I asked, commanding every atom of self-control not to jump out of my seat.

"We found a woman's white glove beside the weapon, in the trunk."

"You did?" I said softly, paling under all my makeup.

"It is the oddest thing," he said, puzzled. "It seemed strangely familiar."

"Don't be funny. A white glove. They're so common."

"Yes, but that one has a little stitching on the back of the hand, made to look like flowers."

Me and my bloody good taste. It'll get me hanged one of these days. If only my mother had been a pauper instead of a duchess of French descent.

"What do you make of it?"

"Not much at present. It's just so out of place. Like a pearl in a plate of peas."

"Where is it now?"

"What?"

"The glove?"

"Why do you care?" he asked.

"Curious about your procedures, nothing more," said I, Miss Innocent.

"That's a first. Usually as soon as I stray from blood and murder, you fall asleep."

"I'm sorry, Barney. Today, I want to know. At least, I'd like to know." I said, pushing my plate away. I hadn't eaten that much. I was more hungry for information than food.

"As far as I know, the boys took it back to the Yard, logged it and locked it in an evidence cupboard."

"Interesting." I said, thinking fast while applying my lipstick slowly. "So, it's guarded."

"If you will. It's on the first floor of the country's largest police station. I would imagine it's quite safe without an actual guard."

"True enough," I said, trying to smile away the clouds of suspicion that were gathering on his brow.

"Why do you care so much about that glove anyway?" he said, putting his arm around my shoulders and his hand on mine.

"No reason. Curious, I guess."

The silence that followed was sizzling. It was painful to me to lie to him. We had a strong bond, ever since we first met. He had led a raid on a squalid dance club I was working in at the time. Part dancer, part lady of the night. It was quite the bottom of the barrel for me. Thanks to him, I was out of work. Knocking on every door, I found the Black Cat and Mrs Huff, which was a true blessing. Not only was I afraid to be found out, but I had leave out parts of the truth. I didn't dare say another word lest I incriminated myself. I was desperate to find a topic which would seem legitimate and distracting enough for him to stop thinking about where he had seen that glove before, or why I was taking such an interest.

George came back to clear our plates but it didn't provide any kind of distraction.

"What were you doing in Shadwell last night, Lucy?" he asked as he sat up, looking into my eyes, all tenderness gone and all my fears coming true.

"I told you, I went with Mary to see Mary's cousin with her," I said.

"Why?"

"What?"

"Why did you go to her cousin? Why last night? What was wrong with her... him?"

"*She* had pneumonia, a bad case. Mary needed support to take care of her."

"Hmhm," he nodded, staring me down. "Why Shadwell, where a murder has been committed?"

"Barnaby, you're incorrigible. I didn't choose where Mary has an ill cousin. I went with her and to Shadwell she took me."

"Don't you think it's an extraordinary coincidence?"

"No, I don't. Shadwell is a dreadful neighbourhood where murders occur often. All the more reason for her to want me to tag along."

"Lucy," he said, his anger boiling under the calm surface, "you seem to forget what I do for a living. I know when I am being lied to. Especially by someone I know so well. I might sound like the dullest boyfriend in the world but I am asking you to tell me the absolute truth, what you were doing last night in Shadwell."

"No, Barnaby."

"What?" he said, backing off the seat, no longer touching me.

"You know my story better than anyone. You are my true friend. In the name of all this, I am asking you not to press me again."

"You're protecting someone. Is there someone else?"

"You do sound like a bad play," I said, "and no, there is no one but another friend."

"A friend? Who do you like more than me?"

"A friend who needs my protection, like I need yours."

I gave him my most pleading gaze, with almost no manipulative intent on my part. And it did the trick. He quickly leaned in and kissed me. I gently bent towards his mouth and my whole body relaxed.

Unfortunately, the moment's peace was interrupted by the chiming of a clock, not too far away. I jumped up and looked at him.

"I am so sorry, my darling," I said as I gathered my things, "but I have to go. I can't possibly be late again."

"All right, go, my little owl," he said as he gave me one last kiss and let me run away.

Having dropped my hat and coat and most of my clothes in the dressing room, I slipped upstairs and in amongst the girls. Mrs Bartlett merely gave me a dirty look and carried on with her rehearsal. Maybe it was the state of my face, which a professional dancer can see under the makeup, or maybe she was just not in a bickering mood.

After the rehearsal, I tried to rest a little and took a nap on a pile of black velvet tabs. Very smelly but soft and in the darkness. Almost like the princess and her pea, I was woken by a little cry from Mary, even more alarmed than the day before.

"Lucy, wake up!" Mary exclaimed, shaking my arm.

I took my arm back with a pained whimper and sat up.

"I am awake. What's happening? Is it time to get into costume already?" I asked, my voice heavy with sleep.

"No, not quite. Lucy, I have bad news."

"What happened? Is it James?"

"Oh, Lucy," Mary moaned, before starting to sob noisily.

"What is it, Mary?" I asked wide-awake now.

"James watched the police take Tiggy and Moosh away, then they brought out the axe, and then…"

She stared crying again.

I tried to sooth her, patting her back.

"I think I know," I said. "They found my

glove."

"How do you know? And how can you be so calm?" Mary said, tears running down her face.

"I met Barney today. He told me. And I know where it is. And I am going to steal it."

Mary looked horrified, either at the thought of my glove left behind or me stealing it. Probably both.

"I lost it last night," I said. "I had to take it off to undo the knots. I couldn't find it, and when you told me I had to leave, I had no choice. I hoped no else would find it until I got a chance to get back. Bad luck."

Mary was no doubt going to ask me the next question, something like, 'How are you going to steal it from Scotland Yard?', when Mrs Huff came out of nowhere and shooed us towards the dressing room. The other girls were getting ready. Mrs Brown was carrying costumes and props to and fro. Mary and I abandoned our urgent talk, hurrying into our red and white costumes.

I was out of sorts all night long. For one thing, that blasted Flora was hitting every mark and looked fantastic in all of Rachel's costumes, which Mrs Brown had adjusted to her more slender frame. The see-through kimono caressed her skin and the Scottish tartan skirt danced over the round cheeks of her backside in the most enticing way. The costume that really seemed to add a shine to her already sparkling blue eyes was the sequined dress for the night's final number, tap dancing like mad on 'Sweet Georgia Brown'. She seemed to fly across the stage. I only had a few glimpses of that number as I had to hurry into my curtain call dress, but I was decidedly torn between admiration and envy.

In another part of my mind, I was considering all the options I had to retrieve and destroy that wretched glove. I blamed my mother for teaching me to be a lady. Because of her, I usually wore white gloves in the summer.

Much to my dismay, my plans were not numerous as the stars that shine. I could sneak in, somehow, and meander my way to the evidence closet, next to the one Barney and I regaled on our last initmate visit. Or I could make Barney show me the damn thing then distract him long enough to slip it in my purse.

Neither were particularly promising.

I had one other option, but that brought a

whole different set of problems. Furthermore, most everyone knew me at the Yard, or at least most of the coppers in the entrance hall, so I would have to go in disguise.

An unlikely plan was taking shape. As I put on my street clothes, I think I might have had a sly smile on my face.

"What are you so happy about?" Jane asked, looking at me through the reflection in her mirror where she was applying lipstick.

Jane had come down from Birmingham the year before. She had been through hell prior to finding the Black Cat and Mrs Huff's daring reviews ('Revuedeville' as she called it in the front page of her programme). She rehearsed dutifully but you never knew what she going to do to the tableaux, her costume or her hair instants before the curtain rose.

"Nothing. It went well tonight, didn't it?"

"Yes," she said, standing straight and looking at me directly, "but you look rough. Are you all right?" she asked, seeing through my makeup and now fixed grin.

"Yes, of course."

"Good. Some of us are going to the Café de Paris. Are you coming?"

"I am hardly dressed for it," I said, opening my coat over my simple summer dress.

"That's not a problem. I have just the thing," she said, pulling out a gorgeous thing of pearls and white silk with tassels and fringes. Quite old fashioned but dazzling. "Try this."

"Do you always have one of these spare?" I asked as I touched the soft fabric and let the pearls run through my fingers.

"I went shopping after rehearsals and that just fell into my lap. Isn't it gorgeous?"

"It's perfect!" I said holding it up, "but don't you want to be the first to wear it?"

"Don't be daft. You're the best of us. You should look like a star."

I was unspeakably moved by what she said. I tried on the dress and it fitted beautifully. Norma, Helen, Tina, Mary and Greta were all gushing around me. Ethel, Bridget and Flora stayed back and looked at us, all smirks, so many snakes preparing to spit venom. It seemed that Ethel had lost Rachel as an ally and had recruited the two new girls to complete her gang. I tried not to care.

As we were stumbling out of the door laughing, we bumped into Barney who had apparently been waiting outside the stage door for some time. All the girls blushed and sniggered whilst he touched his hat and greeted them individually. Much to my relief, his eyes fixed on me and didn't budge, except to notice my dress, perhaps. He didn't care for fashion but he had an eye for detail. The other girls noticed our little world closing around the two of us and made to leave.

The atmosphere suddenly grew tenser as Ethel, Bridget and Flora walked out.

Ethel had never shown anything but contempt for Barney and Bridget was merely polite. But Flora! I thought my whole body might turn to burning coals when I saw her flash her best smile at him. And him, silly man, he smiled back and tipped his hat.

The unease I had felt all night because of my lost glove suddenly faded to nothingness.

How could he? It was to be expected of her, but Barney? He had no business smiling at that tart and her toxic friends.

As I watched them exchange pleasantries, ('Oh you're new in this outfit?' 'Yes, brand new.' Giggles. Blah, blah, blah) I felt my heart racing, my mind incapable of its usual cool reasoning. I felt threatened by that blonde with her soft eyes, so much like his, that I wanted to lay my hands on that axe once more and see what damage I could do. Fury raged within me.

Barney noticed how quiet I had become and met my gaze. He dismissed the armada of daggers flying at him and put his arm under mine demonstratively, bid the rest of the company good night and walked off.

Relief. I was satisfied with the cavalier manner in which he had behaved, cutting her off mid-sentence. I clung a little closer to him.

"That's an awfully pretty dress you're wearing," he whispered.

"Jane lent it to me. We were headed to the Café de Paris."

"It would be a shame to let it go to waste."

"Yes, it would be," I agreed.

"Let's avoid the Café de Paris and make a night of it."

"Wonderful! How about the Ambassador's Club?"

"How about something a little further under the radar?"

"How do you mean?"

"How does The Rochester sound?"

"More than a little under the radar."
"I hear they have a lovely bar."
"Fine by me, as long as you're around."

Since Barney decided to leave in the middle of the night, I got a good night's sleep. Extraordinarily, Julia and I had time to have breakfast together. Her father had given her the morning off due for an obscure Italian religious holiday. We found ourselves sitting together for the first time in a long while.

We had set up the foldaway table and the only two chairs we owned in the middle of our bedsit, halfway between the sink, her bed and mine. We weren't particularly hard up, it was just that neither of us had a knack for interior design, something that mystified Barney. Julia would be working at her father's ice cream parlour until Paolo had set enough money aside for their common future, on top of sending money back home. She knew it was going to be a long engagement but she was getting restless, especially witnessing how I carried on.

Barney never visited when she was home but she found my stockings tied around our doorknob often enough to know we 'saw' each other regularly. Her religious beliefs forbade her to lead such a life, her and half of London actually. We weren't called 'Ladies of Little Virtue' for nothing. We didn't care much for virtue. The high mortality rate of women in London, due to alcohol, disease, childbirth and rough men, led us to live as madly as we could, but fun wasn't high on the priority list of Julia's family so she drank up my stories, along with her coffee. I happily told her about my latest adventures.

"Are you going to marry him?" she asked, her brown eyes glowing under her curly black locks.

"Hm," I said, unsure, "I don't know."

"You love him, yes?"

"I suppose so, yes."

"So you will marry him," she said resolutely.

"Things are not so simple here, Julia. We are free in certain ways that can makes things more complicated."

"Will you still be a dancer after you marry him?"

And with that she achieved something very few people can boast to have done – rendering me speechless. I had never considered the 'relationship' taking such a turn. Was dancing something I did while I waited for the 'right one' to come along or was it a 'career'? I pensively chewed on a blackened piece of toast (Julia had yet to master the art of proper toast).

"I don't know, Julia. We'll see how I feel about him when he asks."

"How you feel?" she asked as if the word was new to her.

"Yes," I said, laughing and getting up to get dressed.

"You are *pazza*... crazy, my friend Lucia."

"I certainly hope so," I said, shamelessly dropping my robe to the floor.

I put on my most responsible looking outfit, a brown skirt and jacket with square pockets. I bought it when I'd been called as a witness at the Old Bailey for a case involving the charge of battering. It was a battle for any woman to press charges, assuming she lived to tell the tale, and for those charges to stick. I had felt it necessary to acquire a conservative outfit that would make me appear a reliable witness. It worked, as the lout was to spend years in prison.

Today I could use it again.

Lucia cleared away our breakfast of pricey

treats I'd bought from Harrods including jam and lemon curd. Meanwhile, I put the finishing touches to my outfit. Since so many bobbies knew me from one or other occasion, possibly at the Yard or even in, how shal I put it, more compromising situations, I had to find a workable disguise.

It occurred to me that these police officers only ever saw me made up, sometimes with stage make up, but always painted. They wouldn't note a dull suited, black and blue faced girl.

They also would take my rape report a lot more seriously if my beaten face was in plain view.

To maintain my reputation, I lowered my head under the brim of my hat while still in our neighbourhood.

Scotland Yard was its busy self. Morning light was pouring in through the high windows on the backs of the bobbies in their dark uniforms. Needless to say, it was a tad warm in the entrance hall, despite the ridiculously high ceiling. The place was crowded with every possible human misery: the battered wife, the impoverished child, the robbed store owner, the beggar boy, the beggar girl, the thief, his wife, someone's abused lover, the drunkard, the vagrant, the malicious criminal, the crafty pickpocket, they were all there.

There were also respectable people here on official business such as lawyers and magistrates. Finally, there were the usual suspects, gents on the dole who had nothing else to do but sit and watch the world go by.

In all honesty, I was a little disconcerted to attract so much less attention than usual, but then I looked a lot worse than I usually did. That was a mere passing thought. I walked as slowly as possible to check the bobbies present behind the counters and pick one I had never met before.

I was rather nervous and not a little bit frightened. Barney, or any of the bobbies who knew me, could round any corner, any moment.

I had been distracting myself with Julia's breakfast and fussing over my clothes, but now I had arrived and the charade had to begin in earnest.

I was almost at the back of the hall, near the foot of the daunting stairs, when I saw the poor soul who I hoped would serve my purpose.

Constable Chester was on the portly end of the police training tolerance scale. He took off his helmet for a moment to scratch his head and I beheld a cute tuft of red hair. His brown eyes were wide and empty. His forehead was covered in beads of sweat which he wiped regularly with a large handkerchief which appeared and disappeared in a flash, as if part of a magic trick.

His discomfort grew when I walked up to his end of the complaints counter and gave him my most charming smile.

"Good morning, constable," I said.

"Good morning, miss," he said, flashing the handkerchief. "How can I help?"

"I don't know how these things go for certain," I said, looking down in deep misery before starting to sob uncontrollably and producing a handkerchief of my own.

"Come now, miss," he said, panic creeping into his voice. "It can't be all that bad."

"You're right, so right," I replied, sobbing enough to win an Oscar or two. " I didn't want to report it but the other girls at the convent school said I should. Men like these should be reported, they told me."

"Men? What happened, miss?" he asked,

some of his professional composure returning.

"I don't know how to say it," I blubbed, looking up at him with my most imploring gaze. "Let me try it plainly, good officer. I was attacked, yesterday, in Shadwell."

I could almost hear his mind whirling into gear. This was above his pay grade.

"In that case, miss, an inspector will have to take your deposition."

"An inspector?" I squeaked, forgetting the meek sobbing girl act of a second earlier.

"Yes, miss, inspectors take depositions, not the likes of me."

"I see," I said, lowering my eyes. "And who will that be, do you know?"

"Pardon, miss?" he said, surprised, then gathered himself, checked a register and said, "Today, it would be Inspector Farringdon."

"Thank you," I said, relieved.

"I'll take you," Chester said as he walked to the end of the elevated counter, opened the wooden gate and led me upstairs.

My plan was jogging along nicely. I don't know why I was worried about the inspector. I remembered that Barney was busy on a case in Wapping.

Unfortunately, my luck stopped there.

In the hustle and bustle of papers being carried and suspects being brought to and from their cells, Chester turned right at the top of the stairs and opened the third door, marked 3, to the right. It was a small room with a table and chair on either side, probably used as much to make suspects talk as to take victims' depositions.

"The inspector will be there in a moment, miss," he said politely. "Do you need anything? Some water maybe?"

"Yes, thank you," I said with crocodile tears still in my eyes. He seemed convinced enough and hurried to fetch me water.

I needed to plan the truly dangerous part of the visit. I summoned my courage and opened the door a little, peeking out. It was busy but not crowded. At any given time, there were about twenty people in the corridor. Most of them were wearing uniforms. Those who weren't were always accompanied. No one roamed the Yard without official business or escort.

I wavered for a moment in my resolve to retrieve the incriminating glove. With it gone, it might become a forgotten, insignificant item and wouldn't hold up the investigation. As it was, they had to find out what it meant in the grand scheme of things. I couldn't let this silly accessory slow down the course of justice, especially for such nasty, violent men.

Also, I did not want to be even remotely involved in this inquest when all I did was right a wrong and expedite matters.

I took a deep breath and stepped out. Hiding in plain sight was one of my specialities. I put on an important business like air and walked briskly towards the door I knew to contain the evidence cupboard, hoping it wasn't locked.

As I walked, thankfully unchallenged, I wondered how exactly I was to circumvent a locked cabinet. That seemed like a very viable issue.

Also, I grappled with the embarrassing question as to why I hadn't thought of it before.

My hair was held up with bobby pins so I could try to crochet the lock but that was not one of my sharper skills. Another option was to fake official business with one of the higher ranking officers. I am sure Barnaby had mentioned them numerous times (complaining, no doubt) but I couldn't remember any names under such a copious amount of pressure.

I safely walked past the stairs and retraced the steps Barney and I had taken a few nights back. The circumstances were vastly different and I wasn't nearly as giddy now as I had been then. I tried to focus my eyes on the handle of the door in question, willing myself invisible to the passing bobbies and detectives.

Much to my surprise, I heard someone whisper, 'Naughty Luce', and instinctively turned around.

I found, standing proudly before me, a young bobby in a brand new uniform and shining helmet tucked under his arm, hair smartly combed to one side. He stared at me with stars in his eyes, giving me the once over, not overly bothered with my dull clothes. He seemed to know what they concealed.

"So it is you?" he said, an admirer of my work, apparently.

"How did you know?" I whispered, oozing artificial embarassment. "I must look a fright."

"Never!" He gushed. "You're the prettiest of the Black Cats, even now."

I shot a reproachful glance at him.

"I've seen you onstage," he said. "You're stunning. You are, miss, truly."

"That's awfully nice of you to say," I gushed back, aware of divine intervention here.

"What are you in for?" he asked with a warming smile, moving ever so slightly closer.

"Well," I said, hesitantly, darting an impressively frightened gaze around. "It's this," I said, gesturing towards my battered face.

"You're safe here, Miss Lucy," he said, concerned, "aren't you?"

"Indeed, I hope so, but the minute I walk out of those doors, who knows?"

"Is someone after you?"

"Yes," I said with a faint, heart-rending sob, "and I fear what he'll do if I don't…"

"What? Tell me. If I can help, I will, Miss Luce," he said, barely able to keep his hands to himself.

"Please, call me Lucy," I whispered very close to his ear, as if choking on tears.

"Lucy," he repeated, enthralled.

"The thing is," I started, my body almost against his, looking up at him through flickering eyelashes, "if I want to get out of this trouble, I need something in there."

I pointed with my thumb over my shoulder towards the evidence closet. He looked over and then at me, raising his eyebrows.

"You want to remove something from evidence? You can't do that, Miss Lucy."

"'Can't' is irrelevant. I **need** to steal something out of the evidence closet and I won't be caught because you're going to help me."

There's nothing like being direct when time is pressing.

"Me? No, I can't do that, Miss Lucy. I just came out of training. I am on probation. If I'm caught, I can forget about my police career. You wouldn't want that, would you?"

"We'll be in there for a second. A second, no more. We won't be caught. Why should we be?"

He hesitated, thinking hard.

"What in the world do you want?" he asked.

"Other than you?" I said, smiling and touching his arm. "A little item, nothing incriminating, nothing that will keep bad people on the street, I promise."

"What is it?" he asked, dizzy from my earlier suggestion.

"The less you know, the safer you'll be," I replied.

"Lucy, you can't expect me to help you with this. To let you in and open the cabinets without knowing what you're planning on taking? Can't be done."

"Anything can be done, if one is willing and able. Trust me, it is not a bad thing. It is a good thing, despite the way it looks. Open the door and it'll be over before you can say Robert Peel," I purred. "Besides, the sooner you let me in, the sooner we can get to know each other. I'll make it worth your while. I can do that, you know."

"Lucy," he hesitated. "I really musn't."

'Can't' had turned to 'musn't'. Progress.

"Sweet officer, help me," I said. "I am not lying. This is a good thing."

He was still diffident. Maybe swaying away from me. This needed a different approach.

I took a deep breath and readied myself to fire a last bullet, hidden in a sugary smile.

"Help me or I shall tell the highest officer present how you know me. In graphic detail."

The threat forced his hand, and his silence.

He chewed over what I had said, looked left and right and made straight for the closet door. I followed him like his shadow.

He opened the door and let me in as if we were having dinner at the Savoy. Once inside, he pushed me against one of the lockers, his hands on both my forearms. It took everything I had not to scream. I knew I had been playing a dangerous game. I was pushing a young man around, toying with his desires. That was always going to be risky.

"You'd better keep your word," he murmured, staring me down.

"Don't you worry about that," I said, right back. "Come and see me after the show tonight. You'll tell your friends about it for the rest of your life."

He said nothing, shoving me against the cabinet one last time.

He turned away and studied the alphabetical letters on the drawers. The shift in his mood had taken me aback. You might think that I would have grown a thick skin, being in this line of work for the past ten years, but I hadn't. I was still shocked when such repressed anger came to the fore and was still frightened of men like this.

Stuck with this roused man in such a confined space, I started questioning the importance of retrieving my glove and had reservations about this unexpected approach. Maybe I should have talked to Barney and explained the situation to him. Maybe he wouldn't have chosen the usual moral high ground and been understanding. Even if he hadn't been, I'd rather be fighting with him in my apartment then silently waiting for the explosive help of this aggressive stranger.

Be that as it may, I was now in that closet and I had to get that glove.

I gave him the name of the suspects and he found the case number on the register. He walked over and used his key to open the drawer.

"Take your pick," he said without looking at the content.

I walked over to the drawer. For a moment, I hesitated putting my hand inside. His hand still rested on the drawer's handle. One shove and I could have a broken wrist. I glanced at him and he smiled as if he could read my thoughts. He took a step back and let go of the drawer. Immediately, I started digging around, looking through rows and rows of paper bags until I found the one referencing my case.

I opened it and, relieved beyond measure to see my orphaned white glove.

I took the paper bag out of the drawer,

straight into my purse.

"What would that be worth?" he said, pushing the drawer shut roughly and locking it.

He walked towards me, his body menacing. With some foresight, I had placed myself between him and the exit. As his closeness grew oppressive, within a moment of becoming unbearably dangerous, I threw open the door and breathed the fresh air of the busy corridor.

I walked from him as fast as I could, looking over my shoulder every few seconds. Approaching the top of the stairs, I bumped into a familiar face, heading up. To my horror and dismay, Constable Poole stood in front of me, smirking as if we had seen each other naked. I'd had the misfortune to meet him at the top of the snow-covered steps of the chess player's home. He had been more than fresh then and it looked like he hadn't changed his ways.

I was once again in the same bind, having to find my away around his intrusive presence.

This time there was no Mary to keep things civil and we were very much on his turf.

I kept moving forward, my mind racing, even more than before, deciding which stance I was going to take with him.

"Well, well, well, if it isn't the bird from the Waverley Street Watch," he boasted. "How are you, my pretty little thing?"

"Dandy, just dandy," I said, keeping a safe distance between us whilst hoping that the other officer had fled, perhaps in shame more than anger. I believed that I brought out the beast in these otherwise ordinary men. A pity, but necessary. And it was their choice. I was not a witch.

"What are you doin' in our old Yard, miss?" he asked, a certain lewdness in his voice.

"Visiting friends," I said casually, heading towards the stairs.

"Come to see me, have you?" he said, as his arm shot out, forcing me to turn around, my back to the stairs. "You're going the wrong way. There are better places to hide."

"Let go of my arm," I whispered, "before you do something you'll regret."

He did not let go.

"I'll report this," I said. "Trust me, I will."

"If you could report me, you would've done it by now," he growled.

And then the voice. The angel on my side. The one that understood me, trusted me, knew my every thought.

"Luce?"

The sound was both the most wonderful and the worst thing I could have heard at that moment. Yet despite these mixed feelings, I smiled as Inspector Cumberland joined us on the ledge of the top stair.

"Poole?" Barney asked with the tone that let you know you'd better have a good explanation ready.

"All okay, sir," Poole said, putting on the most convincing if incredibly daft face I had ever seen. A great actor had been lost when Poole decided to join the London Metropolitan Police. A great criminal too apparently. His ability to lie convincingly was impressive. Or maybe his penchant for reluctant sexual partners was just a bad habit. Either way, he was now under the orders of my boyfriend, and that was all that mattered to me.

"Miss Hall?" Barney said, turning to me.

Ah, there was so much said when he said so little.

"I was looking for the lost property desk."

"That would be downstairs," Barney said. "I'll take you."

An iron grip closed around my upper right arm and down the stairs we went. His jaw was firmly clenched. I could see the muscles on his throat and neck protruding. He was furious, but still managed to talk to me.

"What were you thinking? What possessed you to come here? In broad daylight?"

Whispers. Angry, concerned, puzzled.

"You mean that it's all right to show up at night?"

"You know what I mean. Both for your safety and mine. Oh Lucy, what are you doing here?"

The words almost broke my heart. Such concern, one person for another, was a rare thing.

He gave me a sideways glance that showed me how much he cared.

"I am sorry, Barnaby."

"I know you, Luce. You thought I wasn't going to be here. What were you doing upstairs?"

"Reporting my attack," I said, too harshly.

"To constable Poole?"

"No," I said as I dutifully followed his hurried pace across the hall. "The inspector who was supposed to take my deposition never showed up. I waited in Interrogation Room Three but he didn't arrive. I got up and left."

"And that's when Poole caught you?"

"Yes."

"Be careful around him, Luce. He is dangerous. Not all policemen are pillars of the community."

None of them, probably, I thought to myself, perhaps unfairly.

"He's somebody's relative, in authority, I mean. Nepotism helps."

We had reached the large double doors. A constable opened them for us. We started crossing the wide-open space in front of the building, heading towards the taxi stand when one of destiny's tricks befell me.

I tripped.

This never happens to me. I am a dancer. I have great balance. And yet, under the midday sun, holding on to the arm of my beloved, I fell.

Not just that, of course. Not just that at all.

My purse went flying into the air, spilling its contents as it hit the pavement.

Naturally, the only thing that caught Barney's attention was the brown paper bag, stamped 'evidence' in bold, black letters.

"What is this?" he said, his voice hoarse as, like one, we made for the cornucopia of my purse.

"Nothing," I whispered hoarsely as I gathered the incriminating evidence up against my chest.

"Lucy," he hissed and came closer. "This is one of our bags."

The question was unspoken but clear as the bell of Big Ben. What was it doing there?

"I put it there," I said, certain and uncertain at the same time. Should I be direct? Should I lie? How would he react?

"Why?" he asked.

"Because it's mine. The bag. The evidence in it. The white glove. It's mine."

Barney looked truly flummoxed, trying to understand the implications of what I had just told him. Apparently, our lunchtime discussion had not led him to that hypothesis.

"Don't worry, my love. Believe in me, no matter what. I was at the wrong place at the wrong time."

He stared at me. I could almost hear his thoughts, feel his doubts. I could certainly feel his grip loosen. I took advantage of this momentary lapse and strode away as fast as I ever did, jumping into the first cab of the line, waking the driver.

I instructed him loud and clear, The Black Cat Theatre.

I turned to see if he was following me.

He stood where I had left him, his arms dangling by his sides, his crystal blue eyes looking at me with such disappointment and reproach. No anger, only sadness.

I felt awful. How would I ever explain this to him? Would he find it in his heart to forgive me? I wasn't sure.

I had had to make the evidence vanish. No choice.

There was so much he didn't know about me. How many more of those 'struck dumb with surprise' scenes would we have to go through before all my secrets were out in the open?

This story is based on true events

The Murder

In June 1931, London, a man was discovered murdered under similar circumstances. Two men were arrested, tried and executed.

The Theatre

The Windmill Theatre – now the Windmill International – in Great Windmill Street, London, was for many years both a variety and revue theatre.

The Windmill remains best known for its nude *tableaux vivants*, which began in 1932. In 1930, Laura Henderson bought the *Palais de Luxe* building and hired Howard Jones, an architect, to remodel the interior to a small 320 seat, one-tier theatre. It was then renamed the Windmill. It opened on 22 June 1931, as a playhouse. These simple facts serve only as a basis for inspiration. This is a work of fiction. Names, characters, businesses, places, events and incidents are purely products of the author's imagination.

Cecily Riley, June 2017